Caring for Your Magical Pets

Taking Care of Your Unicorn

Eric Braun

BLACK
RABBIT
BOOKS

Hi Jinx is published by Black Rabbit Books
P.O. Box 3263, Mankato, Minnesota, 56002.
www.blackrabbitbooks.com
Copyright © 2020 Black Rabbit Books

Marysa Storm, editor; Michael Sellner, designer;
Omay Ayres, photo researcher

Library of Congress Cataloging-in-Publication Data
Names: Braun, Eric, 1971- author, illustrator.
Title: Taking care of your unicorn / by Eric Braun.
Description: Mankato, Minnesota : Black Rabbit Books, [2020] | Series:
Hi Jinx. Caring for your magical pets | Summary: Provides easy-to-read
instructions for choosing and caring for a pet unicorn, as well as the
difficulty of grooming the grumpy beasts. Includes discussion questions. |
Includes bibliographical references and index.
Identifiers: LCCN 2018043628 (print) | LCCN 2018052396 (ebook) |
ISBN 9781680729191 (e-book) | ISBN 9781680729139 (library binding) |
ISBN 9781644660928 (paperback)
Subjects: | CYAC: Unicorns–Fiction. | Pets–Fiction.
Classification: LCC PZ7.1.B751542 (ebook) | LCC PZ7.1.B751542 Tau 2020
(print) | DDC [E]-dc23
LC record available at https://lccn.loc.gov/2018043628

Printed in China. 1/19

Image Credits

iStock: id-work, 15 (btm); Shutterstock: Alena Kozlova, 10–11 (hill); alexmstudio,
12 (bkgd); Aluna1, 11 (bkgd); AnggaR3ind, 12–13 (poop), 23 (poop); annalisa
e marina durante, 19 (bkgd); Antracit, 7 (unicorn, paper tear), 16–17 (unicorn);
dibrova, 4 (bkgd); DM7, 4 (unicorn), 19 (unicorn); GCramm, 2–3; gualtiero boffi,
20 (rhino); hanibacom, 8 (rainbow bkgd); helgascandinavus, Back Cover (bkgd),
3, 8 (bkgd), 21 (bkgd); imaginasty, 20 (narwhal); Julien Tromeur, 15 (unicorn,
cupcake); Leh, 1, 10–11 (boy), 11 (unicorn); Memo Angeles, Cover (unicorn, girl,
bubbles), 4 (butteries), 7 (wolves), 8 (unicorns, girl), 16 (girl, bubbles), 16–17
(chickens, pig); MG photos, 20 (fish); MintWind, 16–17 (bkgd); Nguyen Kim
Thien, Cover (bkgd); ONEVECTOR, 21 (unicorn); opicobello, 11 (tear),
13 (tear); Pasko Maksim, Back Cover, 6 (tear), 23 (tear), 24; pitju,
18 (page curl), 21 (page curl); ridjam, 19 (girl); Ron Dale, 5, 6
(marker stroke), 13, 20 (marker stroke); Sararoom Design,
12 (man, wheelbarrow, unicorn), 23 (btm); Tony Oshlick,
12–13 (stink, ies), 23 (ies, stink); your, 7 (clouds) Every
effort has been made to contact copyright holders for
material reproduced in this book. Any omissions will be
rectified in subsequent printings if notice is given to
the publisher.

Contents

Chapter 1
Is a Unicorn Right for You?

A unicorn **gallops** through a field. Its horn glimmers in the sunlight. Its smooth coat shines. The creature slows to eat some grass. After a few bites, it tosses its head and whinnies. The unicorn then races off.

Many people want a pet unicorn. It's easy to see why. They're beautiful, magical creatures. But unicorns are difficult to care for. They can be mean and **feisty**. Owners must know what they're getting into before bringing one home.

Chapter 2
Understanding Your Unicorn

Before you get a unicorn, you must know about them. A unicorn is a large white horse. It has a long, sharp horn on its forehead. This horn never stops growing. It has healing powers too. Unicorns also have large eyes. They use them to spot **predators** in the wild. Unicorns are always on the lookout for danger.

You can tell how old a unicorn is by the length of its horn. The longer the horn, the older the unicorn.

Know the Truth

When it comes to unicorns, don't believe everything you hear. In other words, don't believe unicorn **myths**! For example, unicorns don't like rainbows. They hate singing, and they should NOT sparkle. You should also know unicorns aren't always that friendly. It takes time for them to make friends with humans and other animals.

If a unicorn does sparkle, it has a disease called glitter pox. Stay away from these unicorns.

Know the Dangers

Unicorns aren't just loners. They're also **territorial**. If strangers approach, these cute animals might **gore** them. You'll need to teach your unicorn not to attack. But even well-trained unicorns like to stab others now and then. It's just what they do. So be responsible, and get a horn cover. It's better to be safe than sorry.

Wizards might want your unicorn for its horn. You'll need to protect it from these bad guys.

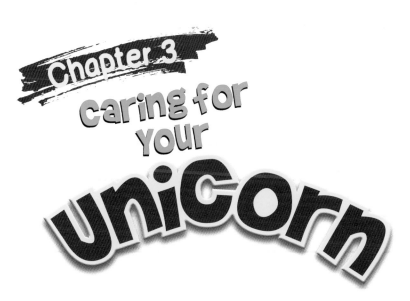

Chapter 3
Caring for your Unicorn

Caring for a unicorn takes time and patience. It also takes a lot of space. You'll need a pasture and stable for your unicorn. You'll also need to keep these areas clean. Unicorns poop a lot!

Feeding and Exercising

Unicorns are magical. But you can still feed them the same food as normal horses. Every day, they'll need hay and fresh water. Apples and carrots make special treats.

These creatures also need daily exercise. They have big, strong muscles. And they love to use them. Give your unicorn plenty of time and space to run. You can also exercise your unicorn by riding it. Only ride your unicorn if it's properly trained, though!

Unicorns are very picky when it comes to letting people ride them. Make friends with your unicorn before hopping on. Otherwise your pet might throw you off.

Grooming

Most unicorns don't like being groomed. But it's something you must do. While they look beautiful, unicorns can smell really, really bad.

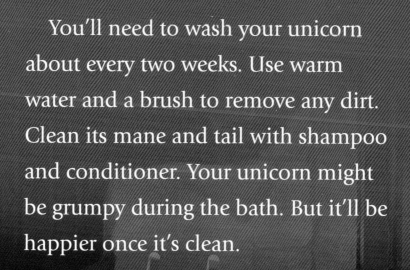

You'll need to wash your unicorn about every two weeks. Use warm water and a brush to remove any dirt. Clean its mane and tail with shampoo and conditioner. Your unicorn might be grumpy during the bath. But it'll be happier once it's clean.

A Lifelong Friend

Caring for a unicorn isn't always easy. These pets need daily care, a lot of food, and space. But unicorns can be beautiful, **loyal** pets. With patience and the proper training, your unicorn will become a lifelong friend.

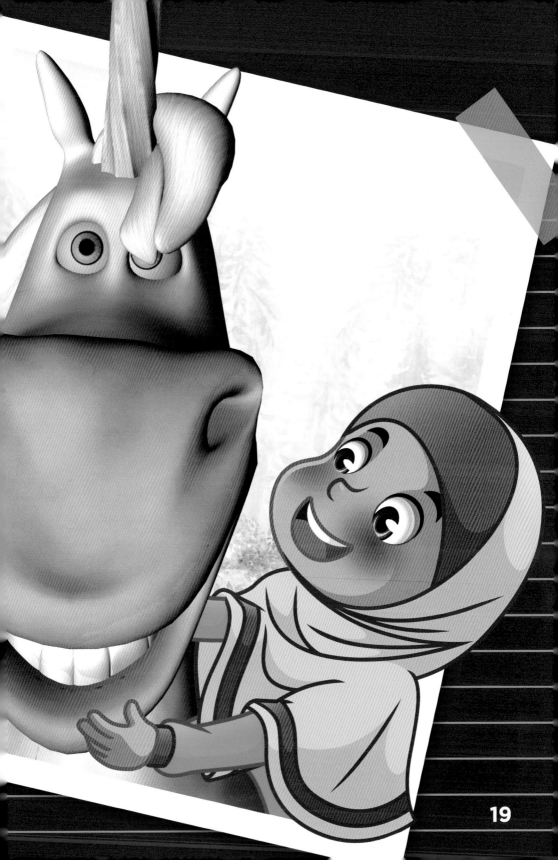

Chapter 4

Get in on the Hi Jinx

There is no such thing as a horse with a horn on its head. But there are some unicorn-like animals in real life. One of these animals is the rhinoceros. Another is the narwhal. A narwhal has one long tooth. It grows through the animal's lip and looks like a horn. There's also the unicorn fish! It grows a spine on its forehead. None of these animals would make very good pets, though.

narwhal

unicorn fish

rhinoceros

Take It One Step More

1. Many people enjoy stories about unicorns. Why do you think that is?

2. Invent a new creature by adding a horn to an animal's head. What is your new creature called? Does it have any magical powers?

3. Would you try riding a unicorn? Why or why not?

GLOSSARY

feisty (FAHY-stee)—very lively and aggressive

gallop (GAH-lup)—a fast, natural run of a four-legged animal

gore (GOHR)—to pierce or wound with a pointed object, such as a horn or spear

loyal (LOY-uhl)—having complete support for someone or something

myth (MITH)—a story told to explain a practice, belief, or natural occurrence

predator (PRED-uh-tuhr)—an animal that eats other animals

territorial (ter-i-TAWR-ee-uhl)—trying to keep others away from an area that someone or something uses or controls

BOOKS

Alberti, Theresa Jarosz. *Unicorns.* Mythical Creatures. Mendota Heights, MN: Focus Readers, 2019.

Loh-Hagan, Virginia. *Unicorns: Magic, Myth, and Mystery.* Magic, Myth, and Mystery. Ann Arbor: Cherry Lake Publishing, 2017.

Peabody, Erin. *Unicorns.* Behind the Legend. New York: little bee books, 2018.

WEBSITES

Monster Myths
kids.nationalgeographic.com/explore/monster-myths/

Unicorn
kids.britannica.com/kids/article/unicorn/390060

Unicorn Facts
www.softschools.com/facts/fiction/unicorn_facts/2517/

23

INDEX